W9-ATG-655

THE MYSTERY IN NEW YORK

created by
GERTRUDE CHANDLER WARNER

Illustrated by Charles Tang

Albert Whitman & Company
Chicago, Illinois

Activities by Bonnie Bader
Activity Illustrations by Alfred Giuliani

Copyright © 1999 by Albert Whitman & Company

ISBN 978-0-8075-5460-9

Printed in the United States of America
12 11 10 9 8 LB 22 21 20 19 18

Illustrated by Charles Tang

Visit the Boxcar Children online at www.boxcarchildren.com.
For more information about Albert Whitman & Company,
visit our website at www.albertwhitman.com.

Contents

CHAPTER 1

Welcome to New York

"There it is! There's New York," said twelve-year-old Jessie Alden. She pressed her face to the window of the train to see the famous skyline.

"How do you know?" Henry, her fourteen-year-old brother, teased. He was sitting next to her and he leaned over to look out of the window, too.

Just then, the voice of the conductor crackled over the loudspeaker. "Next stop, New York City."

"See?" said Jessie.

Both Jessie and Henry laughed.

Behind them in the next row of seats, six-year-old Benny leaned over and whispered to the small dog in the dog carrier on the seat next to him, "We're almost there, Watch."

Watch gave a soft bark. Benny smiled and patted the carrier. Then he straightened and turned to look out the window.

Violet Alden, who was sitting between Benny and Grandfather Alden, glanced out of the window over Benny's shoulder. Then she leaned back and said to her grandfather, "New York is so *big*." Violet was ten, and she was a little timid sometimes.

Grandfather Alden patted her hand. "It's big and interesting and a lot of fun," he said. "Remember how much you liked it on your first visit?"

Violet nodded. "It *was* fun," she said.

"And we solved a mystery, too," Benny reminded her, turning back around.

"I remember. The mystery of the purple pool," Violet said. Purple was Violet's favorite color.

"You liked Mrs. Teague and her daughter, Caryn, too," Grandfather Alden went on.

"Yes. We had fun when they visited us for the Greenfield dog show," Violet agreed. She was feeling better now. "I'm glad she invited us to New York to visit her in her new apartment."

Just then the train entered a tunnel and the city disappeared from view.

"Attention, passengers," the conductor said. "Please make sure you have all your belongings before leaving the train."

A few minutes later, the train pulled into Penn Station.

The Aldens took their luggage from the baggage rack above their seats. Henry carried Watch in his dog carrier and they made their way through a maze of corridors to the information booth.

Suddenly Jessie pointed. "Look," she said. "That man is holding up a sign with our name on it."

Sure enough, a bearded man in a dark red turban and a neat driver's uniform was

holding up a sign that said ALDEN FAMILY.

"How does he know our name?" Benny asked.

"And why is he wearing that hat?" asked Violet.

"Because he's a Sikh, Violet, from northern India most likely. New York City has all kinds of people. And he knows our name because he's here to pick us up. Mrs. Teague arranged it for us. Most taxis in New York will only carry four people, so she arranged for a special car to pick us up, since there are five of us," said Grandfather.

"Six, counting Watch," Jessie said.

Grandfather shook hands with the man holding the sign and introduced himself and the Alden children.

"Pleased to meet you," the man said. "Welcome to New York. The car is this way." He led the way outdoors to a big dark blue car.

"Are we in New York City now?" asked Benny as they pulled away from the train station. All around them, cars and trucks and buses and taxis swerved and honked.

But it didn't seem to bother the driver.

"Yes, you're in the Big Apple now," he said.

Benny eagerly rolled down his window. "Hi!" he cried, waving at the people waiting at the corner.

"Oh, Benny," Jessie said. "Those people don't know you."

"It doesn't matter," Henry said. "See? They're waving back."

Sure enough, the people who were waiting at the corner for the light to change waved and smiled at Benny. Benny waved harder and held Watch up to look at the people. Watch cocked his head. Several more people waved when they saw Watch, and one woman said, "What a cute dog."

"He's smart, too," Benny called out to her as the car drove away.

"This is Central Park," the driver said. "Mrs. Teague suggested I take you on the scenic route."

"Mrs. Teague's new apartment is in a building," Grandfather added, "on the Upper West Side."

The green trees of the park rushed by. Even here, the cars and cabs honked and swerved. Everywhere the Aldens looked they saw people, all different kinds of people.

The cab turned and drove alongside the park. Then it turned again and pulled to a stop in front of a large building. A man stepped out to the curb and opened the car door for them. He wore a gray uniform with gold buttons on the jacket, gold trim on the pockets, and a matching gold-trimmed cap.

"Here we are," the driver said. He got out to help with the luggage. "Have a good visit to the city," he told the Aldens, and with a smile he touched his forehead and made a slight bow toward Benny.

"Thank you. We will," said Benny, and he touched his own forehead and bowed right back.

The driver shook hands with Grandfather. He got into his long blue car and disappeared into the rush of traffic.

Benny looked up at the man in the gray

uniform who had opened the car door. "Who are you?"

"I'm Leed," said the man, without smiling. "I'm the daytime doorman for the building. Six A.M. to two P.M."

"How do you do?" said Benny.

Mr. Leed didn't answer. In fact, he looked as if he didn't approve of Benny talking to him.

"Here. Hold on tightly to Watch's leash, Benny," Jessie said.

"I will," Benny promised. He wound Watch's leash around his fingers. Watch, who thought he was much bigger than he really was, looked eagerly around, his short tail wagging. *New York's not too big for me*, he seemed to say.

"I'm James Henry Alden," Grandfather said to Mr. Leed. "And this is Henry, Jessie, Violet, Benny, and Watch. We're here to visit Annabel Teague."

"Of course," said the doorman. He was a short, stocky man who wore gold wire-rimmed spectacles. "Mrs. Teague is expecting you."

Mr. Leed led the way into the lobby to his desk. He picked up a telephone. He dialed and then spoke into the receiver. "The Aldens are here, Mrs. Teague."

A moment later, he led them across the small lobby to the elevators. "Ninth floor, Apartment D," he said.

He touched his cap and stepped back.

"Good-bye, Mr. Leed," said Benny.

Mr. Leed didn't answer.

When the doors opened on the ninth floor, Mrs. Teague was waiting for them. In her khaki pants and navy cotton pullover sweater, with her red-gold hair pulled back into a bun, she looked almost exactly the same as the last time they had seen her. Mrs. Teague held out her hands, her blue eyes smiling. "Welcome," she said. "Welcome back to New York!"

Benny gasped as he stepped into the hall and looked past Mrs. Teague. "Uh-oh!" he cried. "What happened?"

CHAPTER 2

A Friendly Invitation

In the big room off the hall, sheets covered the furniture. Jagged holes had been punched into the walls. Some of the holes had wires hanging out. Plaster dust coated the room from floor to ceiling.

Just then a skinny man with thinning brown hair and a brown mustache came into the room. He was wearing overalls and a painter's cap that said EVANS' ELECTRIC and he was carrying a hammer. He was covered with plaster dust from his head to his shoes. He kicked up little clouds of plaster dust as he walked. Even his mustache was coated with white dust.

"I have to pick up a special tool from my shop," he said to Mrs. Teague. "I'll be back in a little while."

Jessie stared at the hammer. "Did you make all those holes in the wall?" she said to the man.

He raised one eyebrow. "Yep," he said. He lifted his hammer. "Bam, bam!" he said.

Violet jumped a little.

"Sorry," said the man. "Didn't mean to startle you." He grinned. Then he walked past the Aldens and out of the apartment.

Mrs. Teague laughed. "Arnold has an odd sense of humor, doesn't he? But yes, Jessie, he's the one who made the holes in the wall. Arnold Evans is an electrician. He's been putting new electrical wiring in my apartment. He's done most of the apartment except the dining room, and he's almost finished in here."

"Oh," said Violet. She sneezed.

"I hope he finishes soon so I can put up the chandelier while you are here. It's a

beautiful old crystal one, a real antique."
Mrs. Teague raised a sheet on a side table.
Beneath it, on a blanket, lay a huge chandelier, dripping with crystal prisms of all
shapes and sizes.

"It's beautiful," said Henry.

"When I saw the smashed-in walls I
thought you had been robbed," said Benny.
"I thought it was a mystery."

Violet sneezed again.

"No mystery, Benny," said Mrs. Teague,
ruffling Benny's hair. "Not this time."

Violet sneezed a third time. Benny patted
her on the back.

Mrs. Teague said, "Let me give you a
tour." She led the Aldens through her new
apartment. It was big and filled with sun-
light. A terrace outside of the living room
looked down over Central Park. "Jessie and
Violet, you'll be staying in Caryn's room.
James, you'll have the guest room, and
Benny, you and Henry will stay here in the
study. It has a foldout sofa bed."

"What about Watch?" asked Benny.

"Watch can stay wherever he likes," Mrs.

Teague said. She smiled and shook her head a little. "After all, that's what Sunny does when she's home." Sunny was the Teagues' champion show dog, a golden retriever. She was away with Mrs. Teague's daughter, Caryn, at a dog show that very week.

"Good," Benny said. "Come on, Watch. You can stay with us." Watch followed Benny and Henry into the study.

Violet went with Jessie out onto the terrace at the end of the living room. They stared down at the trees and streets spread out below them.

"Isn't Central Park lovely?" Mrs. Teague said, coming out onto the terrace where Jessie and Violet were standing.

"We drove through Central Park to get here," Jessie said. "It's even bigger than I remembered."

"It's eight hundred and forty acres," said Mrs. Teague. "Two and a half miles long and three-quarters of a mile wide. I go there often. In the winter, I like to watch the ice-skaters, and in the summer there are concerts and plays."

"Do you walk Sunny in Central Park?" Violet asked.

"Caryn or I do every day," Mrs. Teague said. "Or our dogwalker, Lydia Critt, takes Sunny out when we can't."

"A dogwalker?" Violet asked. "Is that her job?"

Mrs. Teague nodded. "She's an actress, too. But she walks dogs to make money. She has her own business, Critt's Critters. She walks other dogs in this building every day, I believe. You'll probably meet her."

"Speaking of walks," Grandfather Alden said, coming out onto the terrace to join them, "I know a little dog who'd probably like that idea."

"Come on, Violet. Let's go finish unpacking so we can take Watch out for a walk," said Jessie, smiling.

A few minutes later, the four Alden children and Watch were back in the hallway waiting for the elevator. When the doors opened on the ninth floor, a short round man with a round face and silver hair was in the elevator. His solemn face brightened when he saw the children.

He looked down at Watch as the Aldens got on. "Well, well," he said. "I don't think I've seen you in the building before."

"No," agreed Benny, who was holding Watch's leash. "We're visiting Mrs. Teague and Sunny and Caryn. But Sunny and Caryn are at a dog show. I'm Benny Alden and this is Watch."

"How do you do, Watch? How do you do, Benny?" the man said. "I'm Edgar Pound, Annabel Teague's upstairs neighbor. I'm sure you'll have fun staying with her."

Henry, Jessie, and Violet introduced themselves, too. Henry said, "Do you have a dog?"

Mr. Pound shook his head. "I'd love to have a dog, but I'm afraid I'm too busy for that. PoundStar Enterprises takes all my time. It's my company."

"Your very own company?" Violet asked.

Mr. Pound nodded. He leaned down toward Benny and opened his eyes wide. "It's named after the Elizabeth Star."

"The Elizabeth Star? What's that?" Henry wanted to know.

Mr. Pound straightened up again before he answered. "A diamond pendant. It was given to one of my late wife Kathryn's ancestors by Elizabeth I, Queen of England in the 1500s," said Mr. Pound proudly.

"So it must be pretty old," Benny said.

"Yes. It's old and beautiful. And lucky," said Mr. Pound. "It's always brought our family good fortune. . . . Well, almost always," Mr. Pound added softly as the elevator stopped. When the doors opened on the lobby, Mr. Pound motioned for the Aldens to go first. He stepped out after them.

"Good morning, Mr. Pound," said Mr. Leed, jumping up from his desk.

"Good morning, Leed," said Mr. Pound.

Mr. Leed hurried to open the heavy glass door of the building for Mr. Pound and the Aldens.

At the curb, a man in a uniform got out of a long black car and opened the door. Mr. Pound nodded at the man and got in. The car began to pull away. Then it stopped.

Mr. Pound's window hummed down. He looked out at the Aldens and motioned for them to come closer. "Would you like to see the Elizabeth Star?" he asked.

Violet's eyes widened. "Really?"

"We'd like that," Jessie said.

"Good. Then it's settled." Mr. Pound smiled. "Come see it tonight. It's in my penthouse."

"Thank you," said Henry.

Mr. Pound nodded. "I'll get in touch with Mrs. Teague to make arrangements," he said. The window of the car hummed shut and the car pulled away.

Mr. Leed, who had been standing close enough to hear the conversation, made a sour face and said, "Now, that's a bit of luck, to get a special invitation to see the Elizabeth Star. They say it's worth millions."

"Have you ever seen it?" Benny wanted to know.

"No. Why would *I* have seen it?" asked Mr. Leed. He turned abruptly and marched back inside to his desk.

"He's awfully cranky," said Jessie in a low voice to the others.

"Maybe he doesn't like his job," said Benny.

"Maybe," said Jessie. She glanced back through the heavy glass door. Mr. Leed was carefully spreading out a newspaper at his desk.

"Come on. Let's take Watch for a walk and explore a little," said Henry.

The Aldens walked to the corner and crossed the street at the crosswalk. They walked until they found an entrance in the low stone wall that bordered the park.

When they got into the park, the noise of the traffic faded. But, reaching the circular drive that went around the inside of the park, they saw plenty of traffic — people traffic! People jogging, people biking, people roller-skating and blading with headphones on, people walking, and people riding in horse-drawn carriages. Vendors sold hot dogs, pretzels, ice cream, and sodas. On benches that lined the walks, more people read newspapers and books or ate lunch. Some people just sat back with their faces tipped up to the bright afternoon sun. One man was feeding bread to a flock of pigeons.

"Woof!" Watch barked as they walked by. The flock of birds swirled quickly into the air and the man laughed and waved. The pigeons landed again almost immediately and went back to pecking at the bread the man scattered around his feet.

"Where are the cars?" asked Benny.

"According to the guidebook, cars aren't allowed in the park during the middle of the day," said Henry. "And not at all on weekends."

Benny nodded. "That's a good idea," he said. "That's what I would do if I were mayor, except I'd make all the hot dogs and ice cream and pretzels free."

"You'd get my vote, then," said Henry, and rumpled Benny's hair.

At a pond where ducks and swans swam, Watch stared intently, wagging his tail a little. But this time he didn't bark.

After they had been walking a little while,

Benny pointed. "Look, Watch," he said. "It's a statue of a dog."

Ahead was a statue of a husky, his ears up, his tail curled over his back. "It must be a famous dog," said Violet, "to have a statue."

They walked closer and read the inscription at the base.

"What does it say?" asked Benny.

"Balto," said Henry. "That's his name. It's dedicated to the sled dog team that took medicine to a village in Alaska and saved everybody in a diphtheria epidemic in 1925."

"A hero," said Violet. They looked up at the statue of the brave and noble dog.

As they walked away, Benny leaned over to pet Watch. "Keep up the good work solving mysteries," he whispered to the little dog. "Maybe one day you'll have a statue of your very own back home in Greenfield."

"Oh, Benny," said Henry. He grinned. "I don't think we're going to find any mysteries in New York City. Not on this visit."

But Henry was wrong, as they were all soon to find out.

CHAPTER 3

The Elizabeth Star

Mr. Leed was at his desk turning the pages of a dictionary when the Aldens returned from their walk in the park with Watch. He didn't get up to open the door and barely looked at them before picking up his pencil and going back to his crossword puzzle.

"Hello, Mr. Leed," said Jessie.

"Mmm," said Mr. Leed.

The elevator door opened.

"Look out!" cried Violet.

The Aldens jumped left and right as five

22

small black dogs with big black ears came charging out of the elevator, panting eagerly.

"Whoa! Whoaaaa!" said the young woman holding on to their leashes. The dogs slowed down a little. Then one of them saw Watch and began to bark. The other four dogs began to bark, too.

"Jim! Jack! Joe! Jill! Jinx! Be quiet!" the young woman scolded. She was a tall woman, with curly black hair, big blue eyes, and a faint scattering of freckles across her nose. She was wearing jeans, sneakers, and a gray sweatshirt that said CRITT'S CRITTERS. Crystal earrings sparkled, dangling from her ears, and another crystal hung on a silver chain around her neck.

One of the dogs touched noses with Watch. He stopped barking. Soon all the other dogs had touched noses with Watch and had stopped barking, too. All six dogs began to wag their tails and make friends.

"Cute dog," said the young woman, leaning over to pet Watch.

"Yours are cute, too," said Violet. "What kind of dogs are they?"

"Oh, they're not my dogs," said the young woman.

"I know what kind of dogs they are," said Jessie eagerly. "I remember from the Greenfield dog show: French bulldogs."

"Good guess," said the young woman.

Jessie beamed with pride.

"And I know who you are," said Henry. "Lydia Critt."

"Good guess again," the young woman said, her eyes crinkling in a smile. "But who are you? Detectives?"

"Yes, we are," said Benny.

Henry laughed and introduced everyone. "We're staying with Mrs. Teague. She said we might meet you," he told Lydia.

"And you're wearing a shirt that says " 'Critt's Critters,' " Jessie pointed out.

"That's me," Lydia said. "Dogwalker by day and actor by night. Only these days, the dog-walking business is better than the acting business." Her hand went up to her neck and she touched the crystal hanging there. "But my luck is about to change. I know it is."

"How do you know?" asked Benny.

"This crystal. It's supposed to bring good luck," she said, still touching it.

The dogs began to pull on their leashes and bark. "Oops. I've got to go. See you later," said Lydia, and she walked briskly out of the lobby.

"Lunch is soup and salad on the terrace," Mrs. Teague announced. "Mr. Evans is still working in the dining room."

The Aldens helped Mrs. Teague and Grandfather Alden set the small round table on the terrace, taking plates and silverware and food from the kitchen through the dining room.

As they did, Benny said, "Hi, Mr. Evans! You've filled up some of the holes in the wall."

"Yes," said Mr. Evans.

"I could help you make more holes in the walls," Benny offered hopefully.

"No," said Mr. Evans. "I don't think so."

He looked as if he were trying not to smile.

Behind Benny, Mrs. Teague laughed. "Why don't you give Watch some fresh water and a dog biscuit from the jar on the kitchen counter, Benny." To Mr. Evans she said, "But I will be able to use the dining room tonight, won't I? We're having a dinner guest."

Before Mrs. Teague could answer, Jessie said, "Is it Mr. Pound?"

"Right. He called and told me about his invitation to you to see his famous diamond," said Mrs. Teague. "He's going to have dinner here and then take you up to see the Elizabeth Star."

"The dining room will be finished," said Mr. Evans. "No problem."

"Great," said Mrs. Teague.

While they ate lunch, the Aldens told Grandfather and Mrs. Teague about their morning. Then Mrs. Teague told them about Mr. Pound's plans. "He wants you to come up and get him before dinner," she told the Aldens. "He's going to be working at his office at home and he *says* he sometimes loses track of time. Truth is, he loves to see children. He never had any of his own. He's been lonely since his wife died a few years ago."

"I'll go up and get him," Benny volunteered.

"I'll go with you," Jessie said.

"This evening's plans sound very exciting," Grandfather Alden said.

"Yes," agreed Benny. "Even if we don't have a mystery to solve."

"Instead of a mystery, how about a museum?" suggested Grandfather. "The American Museum of Natural History isn't far from here and it has everything from dinosaurs to whales."

"Let's go!" said Benny.

The Aldens spent the whole afternoon at the museum. Benny liked the dinosaurs. Henry liked the Hall of Ocean Life, where a life-size copy of a blue whale was suspended from the ceiling. Jessie liked the four-billion-year-old meteorite on display in the Hall of Meteorites. "It says this is the largest meteorite to ever be found on the earth's surface," she said, reading from a small plaque nearby.

Violet couldn't decide which exhibit was her favorite. "I want to see everything before I make up my mind," she declared.

"You'd have to stay here a long, long time," Grandfather told her. "The American Museum of Natural History is the largest museum of its kind in the world."

"Then I guess I like the gemstones best," Violet said. "They twinkle so, like stars of all different colors."

When the Aldens got back to the apartment building, a new doorman was on duty. This one was almost as unfriendly as Leed. He had sandy hair and bushy eyebrows. He narrowed his brown eyes and watched them as they came in.

Once again, Grandfather patiently introduced himself and the children. "And you must be the evening doorman," he said. He looked at the name tag the doorman wore. "Mr. Saunders?"

"Right," said Mr. Saunders. "Two P.M. to ten P.M. shift, weekdays."

He walked briskly back to his desk and sat down.

" 'Bye, Mr. Saunders," said Benny as they got onto the elevator.

"Good evening," said Mr. Saunders.

When they reached Mrs. Teague's apartment, they discovered that Mr. Evans had just finished plastering the last hole in the wall. The chandelier sparkled above the table. Mr. Evans folded up his ladder and propped it in a corner, while Mrs. Teague hurried around the dining room, pulling sheets off chairs.

"Thank you, Mr. Evans," said Mrs. Teague.

"I'm not finished in here," he cautioned. "I still have to paint over the patches."

"I know," she answered. "But it's finished enough for us to have dinner."

Mr. Evans shrugged. "See you tomorrow," he said, and left.

The Aldens went to work helping Mrs. Teague. They dusted tables and chairs, swept the floor, vacuumed the rug, and even wiped the mirror over the sideboard.

Then, while Violet and Henry helped Mrs. Teague set the table, Benny and Jessie went up to Mr. Pound's penthouse.

He opened the door almost as soon as they knocked. "Hello," he said.

"It's time for dinner," Benny said.

Mr. Pound looked at his watch and smiled. "It's six-thirty. You sound as if you are hungry."

"I am," said Benny.

"Too hungry to want to see the Elizabeth Star?" asked Mr. Pound.

"Right now?" Jessie said.

"Why not?" said Mr. Pound. "Come in and I'll show it to you before we go down to dinner."

So Jessie and Benny followed Mr. Pound into his penthouse — the biggest apartment in the building, on the very top floor. He led them across a large living room. One whole wall was windows, bright with the lights of the city far below.

Mr. Pound led them down a long hall

hung with paintings. He paused in front of one painting and stared at it. Jessie and Benny stopped next to him. The painting was of a beautiful woman with a kindly expression and a touch of gray in her hair. She wore a velvety blue dress that matched the color of her eyes. Mr. Pound shook his head gently as though to clear his thoughts and then walked on. Jessie and Benny exchanged glances and followed Mr. Pound down the hall.

At the end of the hall, Mr. Pound opened a door to reveal a deep closet. He pushed the coats aside and then, to the astonishment of Jessie and Benny, stepped inside!

"Come on," said Mr. Pound, and he switched on an overhead closet light.

They followed Mr. Pound and saw a keypad glowing on the wall behind the coats. It was numbered and looked like the front of a touch-tone telephone. The numbers glowed in the darkness and a small red light blinked on one side of the rows of numbers.

"What's that?" Jessie asked.

"An alarm system," Mr. Pound explained. "If anybody opens the door without punching the secret code number in, an alarm goes off here and at the alarm company. They call and if I don't answer the phone to tell them it is a false alarm, they send the police."

"A burglar alarm," said Jessie.

"What door?" asked Benny.

"You'll see," said Mr. Pound. He punched some buttons and a green light came on. "Now the alarm is off," he said. He reached up and pressed one corner of the seemingly solid wood wall.

With a quiet click, a door slid open. Mr. Pound stepped inside, turned on another light, and motioned for Benny and Jessie to follow.

The room was small, not much bigger than the closet. The walls were bare and there were no windows. In the center of the room in a glass case, a large pear-shaped diamond on a gold chain rested on a mound of blue velvet. A single overhead spotlight shone on the diamond.

"How beautiful," breathed Jessie. "It's as beautiful as any of the gems we saw in the museum today."

"It's so *big*," said Benny.

Mr. Pound nodded. "Yes," he said thoughtfully. They stared at it for a moment longer. Then Mr. Pound said, "We'd better hurry or we'll be late for dinner."

When they left, he closed the door behind them. He punched the code into the burglar alarm and the red light began to blink. Then Mr. Pound, Benny, and Jessie went down to Mrs. Teague's.

In the dining room, on the big table under the beautiful chandelier, there was a chicken dinner waiting for them. Everyone sat down. Mr. Pound was in a good mood. He laughed often and complimented Mrs. Teague on the delicious food. He asked lots of questions about the Aldens, and soon they were telling him about living in the boxcar.

"You lived in a boxcar?" Mr. Pound said. He looked amazed.

"Until Grandfather found us," Jessie said.

Taking turns, the four Alden children told Mr. Pound how, when they had first become orphans, they didn't know they had a grandfather who wanted them. So they went to live in an old abandoned boxcar in the woods. They'd had to take care of themselves.

"And then we took care of Watch, too," said Violet. "We found him, with a thorn in his paw."

"And then Grandfather found us," Henry said. "And we went to live with him in Greenfield."

"And Grandfather put the boxcar behind our house and we can visit it whenever we want," concluded Benny.

"That's some story," said Mr. Pound. He put his coffee cup in his saucer and said to Mrs. Teague, "And that was a fine meal."

"Thank you," said Mrs. Teague.

"Now, before we have dessert," said Mr. Pound, "why don't we take a break and go up to see the Elizabeth Star. Violet and Henry haven't seen it yet."

"May we bring Watch this time?" asked

Benny. "He'd like to see the diamond. Wouldn't you, Watch?"

Watch, who'd been sitting politely on his dog pillow just inside the entrance to the kitchen, stood up and barked once as if to say, *Yes*.

"Of course Watch can come," said Mr. Pound.

"Wait till you see it," Benny said in a hushed voice as they stepped off the elevator. He and Jessie had naturally told the others about getting to see the diamond before dinner.

As they crossed the penthouse living room, a clock began to chime. "Eight o'clock," said Mr. Pound. He led the way to the closet. He glanced at the painting of the lady in blue, but he didn't stop. Once again, he punched numbers into the burglar alarm as Benny and Jessie explained how the alarm worked.

"A secret door," Henry said in surprise.

"It's warm in here," said Mr. Pound, wiping his forehead. "Now, the Elizabeth Star is priceless," he continued as he slid the door to the windowless room open. "You can't be too careful when . . ."

He stepped into the tiny room, but he never finished the sentence. The alarm began to clang so loudly that Violet clapped her hands over her ears.

Watch barked and tugged so hard on his leash, he almost pulled Benny over.

Mr. Pound turned, his handkerchief raised to his pale forehead. "It's gone!" he shouted. "The Elizabeth Star has been stolen!"

CHAPTER 4

Broken Glass

At that moment, the phone began to ring. Mr. Pound spun around and pushed his way out of the closet. He stumbled over Watch's leash somehow. Watch broke loose.

"Watch!" cried Benny.

Mr. Pound raced to the phone and snatched up the receiver. "Call the police," he shouted into the phone. "I've been robbed."

"That must be the alarm company calling," said Jessie.

Benny ran after Watch. Grandfather and Mrs. Teague tried to help him catch the excited barking dog. Violet kept her hands over her ears and backed away from the awful shrieking noise of the alarm.

Someone began pounding on the front door.

"Get the door!" Mr. Pound called.

Jessie and Henry raced to the front door and Jessie threw it open. Mr. Saunders stood there.

"What happened? What's wrong?" he demanded. "The alarm went off!"

"Mr. Pound has been robbed," Henry said.

Now Mr. Saunders's bushy red eyebrows shot upward. Then he said, "Robbed? Not the . . . not the Elizabeth Star?"

"Yes," said Jessie, loudly enough to be heard over all the noise.

"But—that's impossible. No one has been in or out of this building all evening except the people who live here and their guests," said Mr. Saunders.

Just then, the alarm stopped. Jessie and

Henry turned and saw Mr. Pound emerge from the closet. He took out his handkerchief and wiped his face again, then wadded it back into his jacket pocket. "The police are on their way," he said. "I just turned off the alarm."

Mr. Saunders crossed the room. "It was in the closet?" he asked.

"In a hidden room behind a secret door at the back of the closet," said Violet, who had just stopped holding her hands over her ears.

Mr. Saunders went closer to the closet and leaned to peer inside, where Benny was kneeling by Watch, patting his head. "There *is* a hidden room!" he exclaimed.

"We'd better not touch anything," Mr. Pound told them. "The police will want to check for clues."

"Right," said Mr. Saunders, straightening up. "Well, I'd better get back downstairs."

Mr. Saunders hurried out. A moment later, two police officers pushed through the open door. More police officers followed, and soon it seemed as if there were police officers everywhere, taking photographs and asking questions.

As the officers talked to Mr. Pound, Jessie went to the secret door and looked inside. The glass case stood on a small table. A switch by the door turned on the light that shone directly on the empty blue velvet inside the case where the diamond had been. The top of the glass case was shattered and glass sparkled on the velvet and on the plain wood floor.

Henry and Violet came up to stand next to Jessie. "No windows," Henry noted.

"No," Violet agreed. "No way in or out except through this door."

"Step aside, please," a pleasant, calm voice said. They turned to see a police officer with a camera. "I have to take photographs of the crime scene," she went on.

The Aldens moved away.

Out in the living room, Mr. Pound was sitting on the sofa, talking to two other police officers. "No," he said as Jessie, Henry, and Violet approached. "No, I punched in the code and pushed open the door and the

alarm went off. That's when I saw the glass case had been broken."

"Maybe the alarm isn't working right," suggested Jessie.

The two police officers and Mr. Pound looked over at her. Mr. Pound's eyes darted back and forth and he clutched his handkerchief in his fist.

"Maybe," said one of the officers. "That's one explanation." She looked at Mr. Pound. "And the last time you saw the diamond was when you opened the safe room earlier this evening?"

"Yes, Officer." Mr. Pound nodded and motioned toward Jessie. "She was with me and saw the Elizabeth Star. So did her little brother."

"Is this true?" the policewoman asked Jessie.

"Yes," said Jessie. "It is . . . it was . . . a beautiful diamond."

The policewoman made a note in her notebook and nodded at her fellow officer. He closed his notebook, too. "We don't have any more questions right now," he said. "But we need to dust for fingerprints and take more measurements and photographs and do a thorough search of the apartment and the common areas of the building."

"Search?" Mr. Pound's voice quavered.

"For evidence, clues. You never know what will turn up," said the policeman.

Mrs. Teague, who had been standing to one side with Grandfather Alden, said, "Edgar, why don't you come back to my apartment for a nice cup of hot tea."

"And dessert," Benny said suddenly. "We still haven't had dessert."

"Oh, Benny," said Violet, putting her hand on her little brother's shoulder.

"It might make you feel better," Benny went on. "It's chocolate cake with chocolate frosting."

Mr. Pound mopped his forehead and managed a wan smile. "Maybe it will," he said to Benny. To Mrs. Teague he said, "Thank you. Maybe it would be best if I got away from all this."

"Sounds like a good idea," said the policewoman. "We have Mrs. Teague's apartment and phone numbers so we can reach you if we need you."

The Aldens, Mrs. Teague, and Mr. Pound returned to the apartment. Mr. Pound sank down heavily onto the sofa.

"Just sit down and relax," said Mrs. Teague.

Grandfather Alden and Violet sat down with him to keep him company, while Jessie, Benny, and Henry went with Mrs. Teague to help make tea.

"I don't feel at all well," said Mr. Pound. "This is terrible, just terrible." He mopped his face and tugged at the collar of his shirt. "Maybe a glass of ice water . . ." His voice trailed off.

Violet stood up. "I'll get it for you," she said.

"Yes, thank you, Violet. That might help," Mr. Pound said gratefully. He shivered and looked around.

"The door to the terrace is open," said Grandfather Alden. "I'll close it." He got up and hurried out.

A moment later, Mrs. Teague returned with the tea tray. She found Mr. Pound standing in the dining room by the dinner table. He looked almost like he'd been walking in his sleep.

"Is there anything wrong, Edgar?"

"What?" he said, surprised to see her. "No . . . no, nothing's wrong. Let me help you with the tea tray," he added quickly.

They returned to the living room.

"Here's your water," said Violet.

"Thank you," said Mr. Pound. "I feel better now." He shook his head. "I just don't understand how it happened. Why didn't the alarm work before, when the thief took the diamond?"

"Maybe the thief didn't use the door. Maybe there's another secret door into the room," said Benny. "Maybe someone sneaked in through that and took the diamond."

"No. There are no secret doors or windows," said Mr. Pound. "I had that room built especially for the Elizabeth Star. The only way in or out was through that door in the back of the closet."

"Have you had the alarm long?" asked Henry.

"Two years," said Mr. Pound. "I have it checked once a year. I just had it checked a few weeks ago. It was working fine."

"Maybe someone sneaked into the room and hid, and then took the diamond," suggested Benny.

But Jessie said, "No. There was nowhere to hide in that room. It was too small."

"And how would anyone get out without setting off the alarm?" added Violet.

"They could if the alarm wasn't working right," said Henry. "And it wasn't. It started ringing *after* Mr. Pound punched in the code."

"That's true," said Mr. Pound. "Someone must have tampered with it." He paused, then said, "The police will know."

"We'll find out," Benny said. "Don't worry. We're very good at solving mysteries. We'll solve this one for you."

Benny had said this before about other mysteries, and he had been right before. But Mr. Pound didn't know that. He smiled at Benny. "That's very kind of you, young man. But leave solving mysteries to the police."

He wiped his face one last time, then smoothed his handkerchief out and folded it up and tucked it into his pocket. He stood up. "Thank you again for all your help. And for the delicious dinner."

"Of course," said Mrs. Teague.

She and Grandfather Alden walked with Mr. Pound to the front door. The children gathered up the plates and saucers and teacups and took them into the kitchen to wash them.

"I don't think Mr. Pound believed me when I told him we could solve the mystery," Benny said. He put a teacup carefully on the counter.

"I don't think he did, either, Benny," agreed Jessie.

"It's going to be a hard mystery to solve," said Violet. "The Elizabeth Star was in a room without windows and only one door. No one went in or out until we got there. And no one went in or out of the building except residents and their guests, according to the doorman."

"But someone did go into that locked room without setting off the alarm. And whoever it was took the diamond. We'll have a lot of work to do, to figure this mystery out," Henry said.

"We will," said Jessie confidently. "We'll start first thing tomorrow morning."

CHAPTER 5

A Taste for Diamonds

"Mr. Leed," said Jessie the next morning when the Aldens came downstairs after breakfast. "May we ask you some questions?"

"Do you need directions to somewhere in the city?" asked Mr. Leed. He had a fresh newspaper spread out in front of him and was doing the crossword puzzle.

"No. We're working on the mystery," said Benny.

"Mystery?" said Mr. Leed. "What mystery?"

"That one," said Henry, pointing at the headline of the newspaper. It said, TWINKLE, TWINKLE, ELIZABETH STAR, WE ALL WONDER WHERE YOU ARE.

"Oh," said Mr. Leed. "Interesting."

"Yes. It is. We were in Mr. Pound's penthouse when the diamond was stolen," said Benny.

"You were?" Mr. Leed looked startled.

"Not exactly," Jessie said quickly. "We were there when Mr. Pound discovered it had been stolen. And we want to help him get it back. So we were wondering if we could look at your logbook. You know, the book where everyone who doesn't live here and isn't a guest has to sign in and out."

For a long moment, Mr. Leed looked at them. Then he pushed the logbook toward them, flipped the pages back, and said, "Here's the log from yesterday."

"We want to look at who signed in and signed out last night," Jessie said. "Between six-thirty and eight o'clock. That's when the robbery happened."

"Go ahead," said Mr. Leed. "I don't know what you expect to find."

"You never know," said Jessie. They bent over the logbook.

Running her finger down the page, Violet said, "Someone delivered pizza to Apartment 6E at six-thirty and signed out at six-forty-five."

Henry took a notebook out of his pocket and wrote it down. Jessie said, "And Lydia was here at six-forty-five. She took the dogs out for Apartment 3W at six-fifty. She came back at seven-twenty, but didn't sign out again until seven-fifty."

"That's a long time," said Violet as Henry wrote this down, too. "Thirty minutes. Hmmm."

"And then no one else," said Jessie.

"Sounds like a quiet night. Saunders was lucky," said Mr. Leed.

The Aldens looked amazed. "A quiet night!" cried Benny. "But the diamond got stolen."

"Oh," said Mr. Leed. "Right."

Henry had one more question. "If you

leave the desk, can anyone come in the door?"

"Of course not!" Now Mr. Leed looked indignant. "We lock the door if we have to leave the front desk. And we're never gone more than five minutes."

"Thank you," said Jessie. She turned and led the way back to the elevator.

"Where are we going?" Violet whispered as the elevator doors closed behind them.

"Benny and I are going to 6E to see if pizza really was delivered there last night. Because if it wasn't, maybe it was just a trick to get into the building to steal the diamond."

"Right," said Henry. "And Violet and I can go to 3W and see if Lydia walked the dogs last night — and why it took her so long to leave. She could have taken the diamond then."

"We'll meet out front in twenty minutes," said Jessie as the elevator doors opened on the third floor.

"Okay," said Henry.

Henry and Violet walked to 3W and

knocked on the door. A moment later, they heard small bodies thumping against the door and the muffled sound of barking. But no one answered.

Henry knocked again, harder. The barking grew louder. But still no one answered.

"I guess whoever lives there has gone to work," said Henry. "We'll have to come back later to ask about Lydia."

Meanwhile, Jessie and Benny had found someone home in Apartment 6E. A sleepy-looking man with shaving cream on half his face opened the door. He yawned when he saw them and said, "What is this? Halloween trick or treat?"

"No," said Jessie. "We're visiting Mrs. Teague on the ninth floor."

"Congratulations," said the man. He yawned again and started to close the door.

"Wait," said Benny. "We want to ask you a question."

"Ah," said the man. "Trick or *question*. Okay, ask your question."

"Did you order pizza last night?"

"I did. Everything, hold-the-anchovies.

My usual from the corner pizza. Why?" Now he didn't look quite so sleepy.

Jessie explained about the missing diamond. "We're trying to help Mr. Pound find out who took it," she said. "And we wanted to make sure that someone really delivered pizza to your apartment."

"He sure did. Leo. He's been delivering pizza to me for a few years now. Paying his way through college. He had to wait while I found money to pay for it. That's why it took him so long," the man said.

"Thank you," Jessie said.

"You're welcome," the man said, and closed the door.

Downstairs, Jessie and Benny found Henry and Violet sitting on the low wall around one of the flower beds outside the building.

"The pizza man didn't do it," said Benny. "He's a real pizza man, not a diamond thief."

"No one was home where the French bulldogs live," reported Henry. "So we couldn't find out if Lyd—"

"Shhh," said Jessie. She waved. "Hi, Lydia," she said.

They all looked up and saw Lydia striding down the sidewalk.

"Good morning," said Lydia. "Can't stop to talk. The dogs are waiting." She hurried by.

When she passed, Henry said, "I know what we should do. Let's follow Lydia after she walks the dogs. Maybe she will act suspicious."

"Let's go across the street to the park," suggested Violet. "We can watch for Lydia there and she won't see us."

So that is what they did. They waited until Lydia had returned from walking the five French bulldogs. Then they followed her as she left Mrs. Teague's building.

The Aldens trailed after Lydia as she strolled along the park. At the bottom of the park she turned left. She walked across to Fifth Avenue and turned right, heading downtown. A few blocks later she stopped to stare into a window.

"Tiffany's," said Jessie. "It's a very famous jewelry store."

Sure enough, even from where they stood, hiding behind a mailbox and lamppost, the Aldens could see lots and lots of diamonds and pearls and all kinds of precious jewels on display in the windows of the store.

"Maybe she is going to try to sell the diamond to them," said Violet.

But Henry shook his head. "No. A famous store like Tiffany's would never buy a stolen diamond. Lydia would have to sell it secretly to someone dishonest."

"Maybe she wants to buy fancy jewelry when she sells the diamond and she is just window-shopping now," Jessie said. "Something even nicer than her crystal necklace."

"Or maybe she's just trying to figure out how much the Elizabeth Star is worth," added Violet.

Lydia leaned over to look more closely at something in the window. Then she straightened up and walked into Tiffany's.

The Aldens exchanged glances.

"Come on," said Henry.

They walked into Tiffany's after Lydia, and stopped.

The whole place seemed to glitter. What seemed like endless rows of glass cases filled the room, each glimmering with diamonds, emeralds, and rubies, along with silver and gold.

"Wow," said Benny, his eyes round.

"Look," Violet said softly. "That lady has her dog with her."

A tall, elegant woman was tucking a robin's-egg-blue box into a Tiffany's shopping bag. Over one shoulder was a large square leather purse and sure enough, sitting in the purse, peering back at the Aldens, was a small, silky-haired brown dog with bright button eyes and a bow on its head.

"We could have brought Watch to Tiffany's," Benny said.

"Shhh! There's Lydia," whispered Jessie.

Just ahead of them, Lydia had stopped in front of a counter and was leaning down.

"Those are diamonds in that case," Violet breathed.

But Lydia didn't stay long by the sparkling display. She stepped back and continued to wander up and down the aisles.

"She's looking at the people in here as much as she's looking at the jewels," said Henry thoughtfully. "It's almost as if she is studying them."

Violet's eyes widened. "Maybe she's planning another robbery. Maybe she's going to see what someone buys, then follow that person home and steal it!"

A moment later, Lydia walked around a display case that glittered with gold. As the Aldens started to follow her, a large man in a dark suit stepped into their path. "Look at this, dear," he said to a woman with a bored expression who stood nearby. He didn't even seem to notice the Aldens.

Quickly, they ducked around the large man, just in time to see Lydia vanishing through a side door that led onto the street.

"She's getting away," gasped Jessie. They

rushed to the door and out—and stopped.

Lydia was gone. She had vanished into the crowds that streamed past them on the sidewalk.

"Do you think she knew we were following her?" asked Benny a little while later.

Henry shook his head. He couldn't answer because he had a mouthful of hot dog and mustard.

"Me either," Benny agreed, taking a bite of his own hot dog. "She never even looked back once. Have you ever noticed how people never look back? That's why they're so easy to follow."

The Aldens were eating lunch. They had bought hot dogs from a park vendor and found a spot on a bench above Wollman Rink in Central Park. As they ate, they watched the people roller-skating and blading in the rink below and talked about the mystery.

"Lydia is our best suspect," said Jessie. "And she *was* acting a little oddly in Tiffany's."

"But that doesn't make her a thief," Violet said.

Henry said, "If she's not the thief, then someone else is. But there were no strangers in the building last night, according to Mr. Saunders. And no one else signed in or out."

They munched on in thoughtful silence. Benny had finished his hot dog and was watching Violet finish hers when Jessie broke the spell.

"What if Mr. Saunders isn't telling the truth? What if he let someone in?"

"Maybe he did," said Henry.

"Or maybe he did it himself," said Benny.

"I don't think so, Benny. He can't leave his desk for very long, because he locks the front door when he does. If he did that, someone would have noticed."

"That's true," agreed Violet. "I don't think Mr. Saunders could have been away from his desk long enough to break into Mr. Pound's apartment, get into the secret room, and steal the diamond."

"What about Mr. Pound? Maybe he did

it. Maybe he took the diamond earlier in the evening and then just pretended that it was stolen when we got there," said Jessie. She paused, then shook her head. "No, that couldn't have happened. We saw it when we went upstairs to get Mr. Pound for dinner."

"Right," said Benny.

Henry finished his hot dog and stood up. "We don't have many clues. I think we need to ask more questions. And I think we need to start with Mr. Pound."

CHAPTER 6

View from the Harbor

Henry called Mrs. Teague from a pay phone on a corner and told her that they were going to Mr. Pound's office to ask some more questions about the mystery of the missing diamond. Then he called information and got Mr. Pound's office address. Finally, he looked in his guidebook and discovered that a nearby bus would take them to Wall Street, near Mr. Pound's office.

"Wall Street is named after a real wall that used to be where the street is today," he told the others as they sat down on the wide seat at the back of the bus. Fortunately, it wasn't very crowded. "It was made by the Dutch settlers out of big wood planks."

"Why?" asked Violet.

"To protect the early settlers from attack," Henry said. "That was in 1653 and New York wasn't a big city like it is today. It was just a settlement with a few dozen people."

"And now it has so many," said Jessie in amazement.

"In a very small area," Henry said. "My guidebook says that the island of Manhattan is only 13.4 miles long and 2.3 miles wide at the widest point."

The bus was driving down a street that was narrow, with buildings so tall they seemed to lean over it. It was almost as if the bus had driven into a tunnel.

"This is Wall Street, our stop," said Henry.

They got off the bus. The men and women hurrying by seemed to all be wearing dark suits and worried expressions.

Most of them carried briefcases. When the children reached Mr. Pound's office, a guard made them sign in at a desk in the lobby. Then they rode an elevator up to the twenty-third floor. They stepped off the elevator and saw a pair of glass doors with silver handles in front of them. POUNDSTAR was written in golden script across the door.

Jessie led the way, pushing open the doors and stopping in front of the receptionist's desk. "We're here to see Mr. Pound," she announced.

"Do you have an appointment?" asked the receptionist.

"No," said Jessie.

"We're here to help him find his diamond," Benny said.

The receptionist raised an eyebrow. "Really?" she said. "And which detective agency shall I tell Mr. Pound's secretary you are from?"

"The Alden Family Detective Agency," said Henry firmly. "We'll be glad to wait."

He went and sat down on one of the plush wine-colored chairs in the reception area. He folded his arms. Jessie, Benny, and Violet did the same.

The receptionist picked up the phone. "Some children who say they are from the Alden Family Detective Agency are here to see Mr. Pound. They say it is about the stolen diamond."

A moment later, the receptionist's expression of polite scorn changed to one of surprise. She put down the phone. "Mr. Pound will see you now," she said. She pointed. "Go down the hall, then up the stairs. He'll meet you at the top."

"Thank you," said Violet.

The receptionist just stared at them.

"What's this? You've found my diamond?" Mr. Pound called from the top of the stairs where he was waiting. He smiled, but his eyes looked worried.

"No," said Jessie. "Not yet."

"Ahh," said Mr. Pound. "Well, why don't you step into my office."

In the office, which had windows that went from the floor to the ceiling, the Aldens sat down in chairs facing Mr. Pound across his large desk. On the wall behind him hung a familiar-looking portrait.

"That looks like the same lady as in the painting in your apartment — and she's wearing the Elizabeth Star," said Benny.

"Yes," said Mr. Pound quietly. "That's my late wife, Kathryn. She wore the Star as often as she could. She always said it was one of nature's lovely things and shouldn't be shut up. She thought everyone should have a chance to see it."

"But *no* one will have a chance to see it again if we don't solve this mystery," said Violet softly.

Mr. Pound looked at Violet. Her words had made him suddenly quiet and thoughtful, and the children waited a moment before speaking again.

"We wanted to ask you a few more questions," Henry said, breaking the silence.

"Ah," said Mr. Pound. "Certainly. Go ahead."

"Does anyone else know the security code?" asked Jessie.

"No," said Mr. Pound. "Only me."

"Do you know if anyone tampered with the alarm?" asked Henry.

Mr. Pound paused. Then he shook his head. "It's very strange," he said. "But the police don't believe that there is anything wrong with the alarm. The security company doesn't think so, either, although they are not so sure. A real expert might have been able to fix it so it didn't go off while he took the diamond . . . but they don't think it is possible. I don't understand it."

"Has anyone else been working on anything in your apartment?" asked Jessie. "Anyone who could have tampered with the alarm or found out the code somehow?"

Again Mr. Pound shook his head. "No. My housekeeper comes in every day, of course, but she's worked for me for twenty years. She's very honest. The police have already cleared her. She was with her son and his wife and her new granddaughter all night."

"Did the police find any suspicious fingerprints?" asked Benny.

"No, Benny," said Mr. Pound. "I'm afraid not."

"Has Lydia Critt ever been to your apartment?" asked Jessie.

Now Mr. Pound looked surprised. "The dogwalker? No. She'd have no reason to. I don't have a dog."

The Aldens exchanged glances. Then Jessie said, "Mr. Pound. Could we go look at the scene of the crime again?"

"The scene of the crime? You mean the secret room where I kept the Elizabeth Star?"

"Yes," said Jessie.

"Well . . ." said Mr. Pound. At last he said, "I don't see why not. The alarm's not on. No reason for it to be." He looked at his watch. "My housekeeper is leaving in a little while, but I'll call her and tell her to leave a spare key with Mr. Saunders for you."

"Thanks," said Jessie.

Standing up, Henry said, "Thank you for seeing us, Mr. Pound."

"And don't worry," Benny added. "We'll find the Elizabeth Star."

Mr. Pound shook his head. But he looked

less worried as he walked with them back to the stairs. "Well," he said, "good luck."

Since they were downtown, the Aldens walked over to the Staten Island ferry and rode it over to Staten Island and back, past the Statue of Liberty. Benny waved at the statue as the ferry went by. They admired the famous skyline of the city, with its skyscrapers and distinctive buildings sharp against the glowing sky.

"New York looks different," said Benny.

"Different from what, Benny?" asked Violet.

"Different from the way it looked when we went to the top of the Empire State Building the last time we were here," said Benny.

"Everything seems to change all the time in New York," said Violet. "It's very confusing."

"Not as confusing as this mystery," said Jessie a little crossly. "It looks different from every angle."

Henry patted her shoulder. "It was a good idea to ask to visit Mr. Pound's

apartment again. Maybe we'll find a clue there."

Jessie looked a little more cheerful. "Maybe," she said. "I hope so."

"Thank you, Mr. Saunders," said Benny as the doorman slid the key across the lobby desk.

"You're welcome. Bring it back when you are finished," said Mr. Saunders, "so I can give it to Mr. Pound. Those were my instructions."

"We will," Violet promised. "We just want to look for clues."

"To solve the theft of the diamond?" asked Mr. Saunders.

"Yes," said Henry.

"Well," said Mr. Saunders. He paused. "It certainly makes this building look bad, a theft like that happening here." He made a face. "It's in all the newspapers. Reporters have been snooping around all day."

"Did you talk to any of them?" asked Benny.

"No! Certainly not," said Mr. Saunders.

He looked past Benny. "Sign out, please," he said.

Mr. Evans, who had come up behind the Aldens, said, "I know, I know," and bent to sign the log.

"Hi, Mr. Evans," said Benny. "Are you finished work for today?"

"For today, yes," said Mr. Evans. "But an electrician is never short on work." He looked at Benny. "That's a joke."

"Oh," said Benny.

"Very amusing," said Mr. Saunders without smiling.

Mr. Evans rolled his eyes.

"Come on, Benny," said Violet. "Let's go to Mr. Pound's apartment."

The apartment was dark and quiet. "It's scary in here," said Benny. "What if the thief is hiding somewhere, waiting for us?"

"Don't worry, Benny," Jessie told her younger brother. "The thief doesn't know we are here. How could he?"

"He could if he was Mr. Saunders," said Benny stubbornly.

"Even if he is Mr. Saunders, he can't do anything to us," said Jessie. But she looked around nervously and all four of the Alden children moved closer together.

Henry turned on the light in the hall, and then he turned on the light in the closet. Just as Mr. Pound had said, the alarm wasn't on. He pushed open the secret door and Jessie turned on the single spotlight that illuminated the room. The glass from the broken case covered the floor.

Henry went over and carefully lifted the shattered glass lid.

"Be careful not to cut yourself," Jessie warned.

"I will," he said, frowning. "Why—" he began.

But he didn't get to finish his sentence.

The door of the secret room slammed heavily shut behind the Aldens.

"Hey!" said Benny. He ran to the door and hit it with his fists. It didn't budge.

"There's no doorknob," said Violet.

"It must have a hidden catch, just like on the other side," said Henry.

But before they could look for the hidden catch that would unlock the door, the light went out.

They were locked in the secret room in total darkness.

CHAPTER 7

Trapped!

"Oh, no!" cried Violet.

"Help!" shouted Benny. "Help! Help!"
He hit the door with his fists.

"That won't work, Benny," said Jessie as
she walked forward and bumped into something soft.

"Ow!" said Violet.

"It's me," Jessie said. "Sorry, Violet."

Violet held on to Jessie's arm. "Benny,"
said Jessie.

"I'm here," said Benny, and bumped hard
into his two sisters.

"Oof," said Jessie.

"I'm *not* scared," said Benny, grabbing Jessie's other arm.

"Good," said Henry's voice in the darkness behind them. "I'm not, either. We don't need light to try to find the secret catch on the door. Remember? Mr. Pound had to find it by using his fingers to feel it."

"That's right," said Jessie.

"I think this is the door," said Henry. "I'm going to start over here." From the sound of his voice, Jessie could tell that Henry had moved away from her.

"I'll start over here," she said. She moved along the wall where she thought the door was in the opposite direction. It wasn't easy, with both Violet and Benny holding on to her so tightly.

Jessie ran her fingers over the cool, smooth wood. It all felt the same. Then she felt something. "I found the light switch," she said. But when she clicked it, nothing happened. The darkness was as thick as ever.

Violet said, "Mr. Pound knows we're here. He'll come and get us if we can't get out."

"Mr. Saunders knows, too," Jessie reminded her.

She felt Violet's grip loosen. Then Violet said, "Benny, come help me look for the hidden catch."

Benny let go of Jessie. "Okay," he said. "I've got both hands on the wall."

"Then run your fingers along the wall and press down and see if it makes the door open," said Violet. "Sort of like a magic door."

"Like a magic door," echoed Benny.

"Remember there's broken glass in the room," said Henry. "Stay close to the wall."

The Aldens worked in silence. For a long, long time, it seemed, nothing happened.

Then Violet drew in a sharp breath. "I think I've got it," she said.

They heard a click — and then the door swung open.

"It's dark out here," Violet said.

"The light in the hall isn't working, either," said Henry, flicking the switch.

Suddenly Jessie let out a little shriek as a

shape loomed out of the shadows.

"Don't shout like that," said a familiar voice. "You scared me."

"Mr. Saunders!" Jessie gasped. "What are you doing here?"

Mr. Saunders looked cranky. "I came to see what was keeping you so long."

"Someone locked us in the closet and turned out the lights," said Jessie. "That's what took us so long."

Peering at Jessie suspiciously through his glasses, Mr. Saunders said, "In the closet? What are you talking about? The closet door was open when I came in."

"Not in the closet. In the secret room at the back of the closet," said Henry, and explained what happened. When Henry had finished, Mr. Saunders shook his head.

"I don't know *how* you managed to lock yourselves up in there," he said.

"We didn't!" Benny said indignantly.

Mr. Saunders ignored him. "And I don't know why you turned off the main fuse in the apartment."

"We didn't," Benny said again, even more

outraged. He paused, then said, "What's a main fuse?"

With a sigh, Mr. Saunders said, "Come on." He led the way through the shadowy apartment into the kitchen. In the kitchen pantry he opened the door of a small metal box and pointed to what looked like a row of switches. "Every apartment has a fuse box. That's the box that controls the electricity that comes into the apartment. If you turn off this main switch at the bottom of the fuse box, it turns off all the electricity coming into an apartment," he explained.

Mr. Saunders reached out and flicked the main switch.

Lights came on in Mr. Pound's apartment.

The doorman looked down and frowned. "And it looks like someone spilled flour in here," he said, shaking his head in disapproval.

"We didn't," Benny said for a third time.

Violet sneezed.

"Mr. Saunders," said Henry, "how did you know where the fuse box was?"

"I've been the doorman here for twelve

years. There's not a lot I don't know about this building, like the fact that the fuse boxes are in the same place in every apartment," Mr. Saunders answered. "Now come on. Let's go. I have to get back to my desk. It's almost five o'clock, one of the busiest times of my day."

Violet sneezed and Henry patted her on the back.

No one said anything as they followed Mr. Saunders out of the apartment.

The elevator stopped. The doors opened.

Lydia Critt got on. "Hello," she said cheerfully.

"Hi," Jessie said. "Where are the French bulldogs?"

"Oh, I don't walk them until tonight," said Lydia. "I'm just here to meet a new dog-walking client." She touched the crystal that glinted at her neck. "See? This crystal *does* bring good luck."

The doors opened again at Mrs. Teague's floor. "See you later," Lydia said.

"Yes," said Henry.

"Wait a minute," said Mr. Saunders. He

held out his hand. "The key to Mr. Pound's apartment, please."

Henry gave him back the key.

When the elevator door had closed, Violet said, "I don't think he believed anything we said."

"Or maybe he was only pretending he didn't," said Henry.

"Well, if he's just pretending to be cranky, too, he's doing a very good job," said Jessie.

"Maybe Mr. Saunders is the one who locked us in the secret room. Maybe he followed us upstairs and closed the door and turned off the lights," Henry answered.

Violet said slowly, "If he did it, he must have been trying to scare us."

"Not me," Benny crowed. "He didn't scare me."

"That's right," said Jessie. "And the only reason he would want to scare us is to try to keep us from solving the mystery."

"Does that mean Mr. Saunders is the thief?" asked Benny.

"He's the only one besides Mr. Pound

who knew where we were," said Violet.

"Unless Lydia knew, somehow," said Jessie. "Maybe, if she and Mr. Saunders are working together, he told her and she went up and locked us in the secret room and turned off the lights."

"That's right!" said Violet. "Lydia could have done it. And then Mr. Saunders could have come up to save us, so we wouldn't suspect him."

"Or it could have been someone else who also knew where we were," said Henry. He stopped in front of the door to Mrs. Teague's apartment and fumbled in his pocket for the key. "Someone who would know where to find an electric fuse box."

"Who?" asked Benny.

"Think, Benny," said Henry. "Who else was standing at the front desk, signing out, when we got the key for Mr. Pound's apartment?"

Benny's eyes grew round. "Mr. Evans!" he cried.

At that moment, the door of Mrs. Teague's apartment swung open.

"Mr. Evans!" gasped Violet.

Had he heard them? He didn't seem to have. He smiled. "Hello again," he said. To Mrs. Teague, who was holding the door for him, he said, "Silly of me to have forgotten my tools like that. Well, see you tomorrow."

"You *will* be finished tomorrow, won't you?" asked Mrs. Teague.

"Oh, yes," said Mr. Evans. "Don't worry."

He nodded pleasantly at the Aldens and walked down the hall toward the elevator.

"What's Mr. Evans doing here?" asked Henry.

"He came back. He forgot some of his tools," said Mrs. Teague.

The Aldens exchanged glances. Was that the reason Mr. Evans had come back? Or was it only an excuse so that he could sneak upstairs and lock them in the secret room?

Shortly after dinner, they heard a knock at the door.

Mrs. Teague opened it and said in a surprised voice, "Edgar Pound. Come in."

"I hope I'm not interrupting anything," said Mr. Pound. "I came to see if our young detectives had any luck finding new clues in the apartment this afternoon."

He smiled at the Aldens.

"No luck yet," said Jessie.

"Oh," said Mr. Pound. "Too bad." But he didn't sound very sorry.

"Have the police had any luck?" asked Henry.

"No. Not yet," said Mr. Pound. "I'm beginning to think the Elizabeth Star is gone forever." He took out his handkerchief and mopped his forehead.

"Sit down and join us for a cup of tea," said Mrs. Teague.

"Thank you. I think I will," said Mr. Pound. He started toward the dining room.

"Why don't we sit in the living room," suggested Mrs. Teague. "It'll be more comfortable."

After they had finished their tea, Mr. Pound stood up. Holding his teacup in his hand, he began to walk through the dining room to the kitchen.

"I'll take your cup for you, Mr. Pound," offered Henry.

"Oh, no. No, I'm fine," said Mr. Pound, holding on to the cup.

"But — "

Mr. Pound ignored Henry. He marched into the kitchen and put the cup down. Henry went back to help gather up the rest of the cups and saucers.

He reached the dining room to find Mr. Pound holding one of the dining room chairs, which he pulled out from the table.

"Mr. Pound?" said Henry.

"Oh!" Mr. Pound jumped. "I just thought I'd sit down for a moment." He sat down.

"Are you all right, Edgar?" asked Mrs. Teague, bustling into the dining room.

"I'm fine. Don't worry about me. Just go on and do what you were doing," insisted Mr. Pound.

The Aldens cleared away the dishes, walking back and forth as Mr. Pound sat in the dining room chair.

When Benny had finished helping, he sat down in a dining room chair across from Mr. Pound.

"What are you doing, Benny?" asked Violet.

"Keeping Mr. Pound company so he doesn't get lonely," said Benny.

"You don't need to do that, Benny," said Mr. Pound.

"It's okay," said Benny.

Mr. Pound stood up. "Well, I'd better be going," he said. "Thank you for the tea."

When he had left, Mrs. Teague shook her head. "Poor Edgar. I'm afraid the loss of the diamond has upset him. He's not himself. In fact, I think he looks worse tonight than on the evening of the theft."

"He was acting kind of weird," said Henry.

"Well, we'll find the diamond and then he'll feel better," said Benny.

"I hope you're right, Benny," said Jessie. "I hope you're right."

CHAPTER 8

The Chase

The next morning, Jessie leaned on the railing of the balcony and peered down. People scurried by on the street below. She sighed. "Too many people," she muttered.

"Too many people? In New York?" teased Henry, who was sitting in a chair nearby. At the small table, Violet was reading the newspaper to Benny.

"Read it again," said Benny. "About the diamond."

"It just says there are no new clues, Benny," Violet said.

"And too many suspects," said Jessie. "That's what I meant."

Violet and Benny looked up. "Too many?"

"Lydia, Mr. Evans, Mr. Saunders, Mr. Leed," said Jessie. "Or Lydia and Mr. Saunders working together, or Lydia and Mr. Evans, or Mr. Evans and Mr. Saunders."

"That's a lot of possibilities," agreed Henry.

"Seven," said Benny, who'd been counting on his fingers. "And Mr. Pound. Eight."

"Okay. And Mr. Pound," said Jessie. "Maybe he *did* have something to do with it."

"Eight," said Benny. "And Mr. Pound and Lydia. And Mr. Pound and Mr. Evans. And Mr. Pound and Mr. Saunders. Eleven ways the diamond could have been taken in all."

At that moment, the phone rang. It was Mr. Leed, saying that Mr. Evans was on his way up to the apartment.

"You're early today," said Mrs. Teague when she let Mr. Evans in.

"I woke up early," said Mr. Evans. "And

I believe an electrician should go with the current. That's a joke."

Mrs. Teague smiled.

"Anyway, I've got work to do," said Mr. Evans.

"We have work to do, too," said Henry.

"Are you going to look for clues to the mystery of the missing diamond?" asked Grandfather.

Mr. Evans looked up. "I saw a picture of it in the newspaper. Nice-looking little gem. Gave me a real charge. That's a joke."

"Oh," said Jessie. She looked at her watch. "Well, we'd better go."

Quickly the Aldens helped clear away the breakfast dishes and clean up. Then they hurried out the door.

They reached the sidewalk in front of the building just in time to see Lydia Critt hurrying down the street. She was wearing jeans and a green sweatshirt that said CRITT'S CRITTERS, and was carrying a very large backpack.

"Come on!" said Jessie. They raced after Lydia.

Today, Lydia walked into one of the big hotels at the bottom of the park. The Aldens followed her in. People with suitcases and briefcases filled the lobby. The children saw Lydia vanish down a hallway. But when they reached the hallway, she was gone.

"She must have gone into the bathroom," said Jessie.

"There's no door at the end of the hall," said Henry. "She'll have to come back out the way she came in. We'll wait in the lobby."

The Aldens found the perfect seat, on a small sofa in the corner behind a potted plant. They took turns peering out between its leaves.

Lydia was gone for a long time. When she came back out into the lobby, they saw why. They almost didn't recognize her.

She had completely changed clothes. She was wearing a dress, high heels, a big hat with a flower on it, and she had on gloves. The only thing that was the same was the backpack she was carrying. Earrings flashed at her earlobes, and Violet gave a little gasp when she saw the twinkle of light at Lydia's throat.

"The diamond?" she gasped.

"No," Henry whispered. "It's the crystal she always wears."

"Why did she change clothes?" Jessie wanted to know. "Do you think she knew we were following her and is trying to throw us off?"

"Maybe," said Henry.

"We'll have to be extra careful now," said Benny.

This time, when they followed Lydia out onto the street, they crossed to the other side.

And this time, Lydia kept stopping to look back. Every time she did, the Aldens pretended to be shopping, staring into the store windows.

"She *does* know we're following her," said Violet.

Suddenly Lydia threw up her hand and jumped out into the street. A yellow car swerved toward her.

Violet clamped her hands over her eyes.

"Oh, no!" cried Jessie, springing forward. "That car is going to hit Lydia!"

But it didn't. It screeched to a stop right beside her and the Aldens realized that the yellow car was a taxicab.

As the door of the cab slammed, Jessie jumped to the curb and threw up her hand.

"Jessie! What are you doing?" asked Henry.

Another yellow cab screeched to the curb and stopped.

"Get in!" Jessie panted. Then she leaned forward and said to the driver, "Follow that cab!"

They sped through the streets of Manhattan so quickly that the stores and people lining the sidewalks blurred as they went by. Then the cab turned and turned again. Now the streets were lined with theaters.

"Times Square," said Henry. "Broadway and the Theater District."

Ahead of them, Lydia's cab pulled to the curb.

"Stop here," Jessie said. "At the corner."

Quickly they paid the driver and got out just as Lydia hurried across the sidewalk. She stopped at a door and touched the crystal at her throat.

"For luck," whispered Violet almost to herself.

Then Lydia took a deep breath, opened the door, and disappeared inside.

The Aldens raced up to the door and stopped.

Then Henry read the sign posted on the door. " 'Auditions today for *Diamonds and Hearts*. A new mystery about stolen jewels . . . and love.' "

Then Henry began to laugh.

"What's so funny?" Benny said.

"She isn't a thief," said Henry, laughing harder. "She's an actress!"

Now Violet was smiling. "That's why she put on those funny clothes, isn't it?" she asked.

"Why?" asked Benny.

"Of course! Because she was going to an audition," said Jessie.

"What's an audition?" asked Benny. By now he was *very* confused.

"You remember when we were in that play, Benny. An audition is when you try out for a part in a show," explained Violet.

"Oh. So she wasn't in disguise. She was dressed up for the play," said Benny.

"Right, Benny," said Henry.

"And that's why she was in Tiffany's!" Jessie exclaimed suddenly. "What better place to do research about a play called *Diamonds and Hearts*? She was studying the way the other people were dressed in Tiffany's, too. That's how she is dressed today — like some of those people at Tiffany's."

"With her crystal necklace for a diamond," said Benny.

"You're right," said Henry.

"Does that mean she's not the thief?" asked Benny. He sounded a little relieved.

"Well, she could still be a thief," said Jessie. "But somehow, I don't think so. I think she's too busy to be a thief!"

Henry had managed to stop laughing. "Well, we might as well walk back to Mrs. Teague's," he said.

As they walked back uptown, they talked about the mystery.

"I'm glad it's not Lydia," said Benny. "I like her. And so does Watch. Because she likes dogs."

"Me, too," admitted Jessie.

"But if it isn't Lydia, who is it?" asked Violet.

"Maybe Mr. Pound did it," said Benny suddenly. "Maybe he's just pretending the diamond is stolen."

"Maybe, Benny," said Henry. "But remember, he'd have to know an awful lot about alarm systems."

"That's true," said Benny.

Violet said, "What about Mr. Saunders, the doorman? He could have let someone in without making them sign in."

"That's true, too," agreed Jessie. "I definitely think we should keep Mr. Saunders as a suspect."

"Don't forget Mr. Evans," said Henry.

"Why Mr. Evans?" asked Violet.

"Because he's an electrician. He could probably figure out how to tamper with an alarm so that no one could tell," said Henry.

"Do you think he broke into Mr. Pound's apartment and took the diamond?" asked Benny.

"But the lock on the door of Mr. Pound's apartment hadn't been broken," objected Henry. "The police said so."

"Maybe we should ask Lydia," said Benny.

"Ask Lydia what?" said Jessie, puzzled.

"About diamonds," said Benny. "She's in a play about stolen diamonds. And she has a lucky diamond necklace. . . . I mean, a *crystal* necklace."

Jessie stared at Benny. And then her mouth dropped open. "That's it, Benny! That's it!"

CHAPTER 9

No Joke

"What?" said Benny.

"Remember what you said, Benny?" said Jessie. "About Lydia's crystal necklace?"

"The one like a diamond?" asked Benny.

"Yes!" cried Jessie. "The crystal that Lydia wears for luck is like a diamond. Think, Benny. Where else have we seen crystals like diamonds? Lots of them."

Benny frowned.

Violet gasped. "The chandelier!"

Henry said, "You're right. Mrs. Teague's

chandelier. But what does that have to do with anything?"

"Because I think the Elizabeth Star is hidden there. And all we have to do to catch the thief is find out who hid it," said Jessie.

"In the chandelier?" asked Benny. "The diamond is hidden in the chandelier?"

"Yes," said Jessie.

"Let's go!" cried Henry.

They raced back to Mrs. Teague's apartment and ran past Mr. Leed.

"Where's the fire?" asked Mr. Leed, startled, as they ran by.

"No fire," Henry managed to say. "Diamonds."

The elevator seemed to take forever to get down to the lobby. Suddenly Henry pointed at the stairs. "Come on. That'll be faster," he said.

They began to run up the long flights of stairs. By the time they reached the ninth floor, they were all gasping for breath. As they burst into the hall, they heard the elevator doors closing.

But they didn't stop. They ran to Mrs. Teague's apartment.

Jessie led the way into the dining room. She pulled out a chair and jumped up on it. "It's not there," she said.

"Jessie? What's wrong?" asked Mrs. Teague, coming out of her study down the hall.

Then she said, "Doesn't the chandelier look nice? Mr. Evans noticed how dusty it had gotten and gave it a good cleaning."

"Mr. Evans? Where is he?" Violet looked around wildly.

"He just this second left. I'm surprised you didn't see him in the hall," began Mrs. Teague.

"The elevator!" exclaimed Henry.

Jessie jumped from the chair and, without waiting to give Mrs. Teague an explanation, the children raced out of the apartment.

This time they ran down the stairs so fast that Benny felt dizzy.

"Mr. Evans!" cried Jessie as they burst into the lobby. "Where is he?"

"He just left," said Mr. Leed.

"Which way did he go?" asked Henry.

"Turned left. He might have parked his truck around the corner. You can't park out front, you know. That's for taxis and — "

They didn't wait to hear the rest. They raced out of the building and down the sidewalk. Feet pounding the cement, they ran around the corner.

"There!" Jessie pointed.

A blue truck with the words EVANS' ELECTRIC painted on the side was parked just up ahead and Mr. Evans was walking toward it with his car keys in his hand.

Henry didn't hesitate. He ran and jumped right in front of the driver's-side door. Violet, Benny, and Jessie ran and stood behind Mr. Evans so he couldn't escape.

Mr. Evans put his hands on his hips. "Hey. What's going on?" he demanded.

"I think you know," said Jessie. She held out her hand. "The diamond, please."

"Diamond? What diamond? I don't know what you're talking about." Mr. Evans raised his voice. "Move!" he called to Henry.

Henry folded his arms and shook his head.

"You have the Elizabeth Star," said Jessie. "We know you do."

"Ha!" said Mr. Evans. "Very funny. Get out of my way or I'll call the police."

"Call them," said Jessie. "And tell them how you took the Elizabeth Star from its hiding place in Mrs. Teague's chandelier."

Mr. Evans dropped his arms to his sides. There was a long silence.

"No police," he said.

"Where's the diamond?" Benny asked.

Slowly, Mr. Evans reached into his shirt pocket and took out an old piece of cloth spattered with paint. He unwrapped it and held it out. There in his hand glittered the Elizabeth Star.

"I knew it," breathed Jessie.

"You stole it!" Benny said. "You stole the Elizabeth Star."

"No!" cried Mr. Evans. "I didn't."

"Then how did you know it was there?"

asked Violet. She sneezed, and stepped back a little.

"I was working up on the ladder yesterday morning and I saw it. But there was no way I could get to it without arousing suspicion. Mrs. Teague or Mr. Alden or someone was always around. Anyway, I figured it was safe and I could leave it there until I finished work."

"You didn't steal it and put it there?" asked Jessie.

"No!" said Mr. Evans. "But seeing it there gave me quite a shock, I can tell you." He managed a feeble smile. "And that's no joke."

Violet sneezed again and said, "You make me sneeze. It's the dust."

Mr. Evans gave her a puzzled look.

"It was you," said Violet. "You're the one who locked us in the secret room. And you left dust all over Mr. Pound's apartment."

"Yeah, well, I didn't mean to hurt you. Just scare you a little. Keep you from figuring out where the diamond was until I could get it safely away from Mrs. Teague's apartment," said Mr. Evans.

"Well, it didn't scare us. Not one bit," declared Benny.

"Mr. Saunders didn't tell you to go up and scare us?" asked Violet.

"No," said Henry, before Mr. Evans could answer.

"No," said Mr. Evans. "What has Mr. Saunders got to do with anything?"

"No. No, I don't think it was Mr. Saunders. And I don't think it was Lydia," Henry went on.

"I don't know what you're talking about now," complained Mr. Evans.

"Me either," said Benny.

"I think I know who took the diamond and hid it in the chandelier. Now all we have to do is set a trap and catch the thief . . . with your help, Mr. Evans," Henry added.

"Help you?" said Mr. Evans.

"Yes," said Henry. "And if you do, maybe the police will go easier on you."

"Plug me in," said Mr. Evans. His smile

was a little more genuine now. "That was a joke."

"Mr. Pound, come in," said Mrs. Teague.

"What's this? The children visiting you have actually found the diamond?" said Mr. Pound. Out came his handkerchief. He mopped his face.

"Did I say that when I called? I'm sorry. I should have said they found some new clues," said Mrs. Teague.

"Oh," said Mr. Pound. He sounded relieved. "Where are they?"

"They had to go to the store to get some more dog food for Watch," said Mrs. Teague. "Their grandfather went with them. I'm here by myself, except for Mr. Evans, at the moment."

"Mr. Evans?" asked Mr. Pound.

"The electrician. But he's out drinking a cup of coffee in the kitchen," said Mrs. Teague.

Crouched behind the kitchen door, Violet whispered, "Do you think he believes Mrs. Teague?"

"Shhh," warned Jessie.

"Shhh," Benny said to Watch, tightening his hold on the dog's collar.

"Why don't you sit in the dining room and . . . Oh, dear, I hear the phone ringing in my study. You just sit right here and I'll be right back." Mrs. Teague pulled out a chair, nodded at Mr. Pound, and hurried out of the dining room.

She was barely out of sight down the hall before Mr. Pound jumped to his feet. He climbed onto the chair and stretched his arm up toward the chandelier. He frowned. He leaned sideways and peered at the rows of dangling crystals.

"It's got to be here," he muttered.

"Now," said Jessie.

Mr. Evans pushed open the kitchen door and walked into the dining room, letting the door almost close behind him. He looked up at Mr. Pound. Mr. Pound looked down at him.

"Looking for something?" said Mr. Evans.

"I, er . . . well," said Mr. Pound.

"You know," said Mr. Evans, "I'm an

electrician, and while I was wiring the dining room, I noticed something very interesting about that chandelier."

"What?" said Mr. Pound.

"This," said Mr. Evans, pulling the Elizabeth Star out of his pocket.

"That's the Elizabeth Star," said Mr. Pound. He grew very pale.

"I wondered how it got up there," said Mr. Evans.

"That's mine," said Mr. Pound, getting down off the chair. "You must give it to me."

"I think I should give it to the police. Maybe there's a reward," said Mr. Evans.

Mr. Pound took out his handkerchief and wiped his face. He looked ill. "No need to do that," he said. "Yes, I hid the Star. And I'd like it to stay hidden. I couldn't bear to lose it."

"Go on," said Mr. Evans.

"So maybe we could make a deal," said Mr. Pound.

"And maybe not," said Henry, pushing open the kitchen door.

CHAPTER 10

A Thief's Regret

"You!" Mr. Pound staggered back as the children came out of the kitchen and Mrs. Teague and Grandfather Alden came in from the living room. "What are you doing here?"

"Catching a thief," said Jessie. "A thief who stole from himself."

Mr. Pound looked around wildly. For a moment, it seemed as if he might try to run out the door. Watch growled a little under his breath.

Then Mr. Pound collapsed onto the

chair. "It's true. It's all true. I'm sorry I deceived you all. My company . . . it's in trouble. I thought if the Elizabeth Star disappeared, I could collect the insurance. And I would still get to keep it. It was my wife's. It's all I have left of her. I couldn't bear to let it go."

"That was wrong," said Benny.

"I know," said Mr. Pound.

"No one tampered with the alarm," said Henry. "You must have punched in the right code to open the door, then reset it and punched in the wrong code. That's why the alarm went off."

Mr. Pound nodded. "And then I broke the glass case and took the diamond. The sound of the alarm covered the sound of the breaking glass and no one noticed what I was doing in all the confusion."

"Where did you hide it?" asked Violet.

Mr. Pound held up his handkerchief. "In here. I wrapped the handkerchief around my hand to break the glass. Then I wrapped the star inside the handkerchief."

"And then, when you were downstairs,

you hid the diamond in the chandelier," said Jessie.

"Yes. I thought of that at dinner. It seemed like a brilliant idea at the time. I had no idea how hard it would be to get the diamond back. . . ." His voice trailed off.

"That's why you kept sitting in the dining room the other day," said Benny. "You were going to take the diamond back. But *I* stopped you."

"Yes, you did," said Mr. Pound. He sighed heavily. "I didn't mean to do this. I had been planning to sell the Elizabeth Star to save my business, but the thought of losing it made me so terribly sad. It was Kathryn's, you see. It's all I have left of her."

Mr. Pound stared into space a moment before he went on. "But after I met you children in the elevator and invited you to come see the Star, the idea came to me: If I could fool the police into thinking the Star was stolen, I could save my business with the insurance payment and still keep the Star. I thought you'd be the perfect witnesses. After all, you were just children. You wouldn't notice what was really going on."

"But we did," said Jessie.

"Because we're children *and* detectives," said Benny. "Very good detectives."

"That's true," said Mrs. Teague. "If you'd asked me, I could have told you. After all, I was there when the Aldens solved the mystery at the dog show."

"Mr. Pound," Violet said softly, "may I ask you something?"

"Of course, Violet. I owe you that at least."

"You tried to keep the Star hidden and all to yourself, but didn't you tell us your wife wanted people to see it? That she wanted to share it?"

"That's very true, Violet."

"Well, I know a place where lots of people would see it — the Museum of Natural History, with the other beautiful gems."

"And there are lots of kids there," said Benny. "Mrs. Teague told us you liked children."

Mrs. Teague looked embarrassed, but Benny went right on talking. "And the museum's so close you could visit the Elizabeth Star whenever you wanted to and you could see all those children, too."

Mr. Evans put the diamond on the table in front of Mr. Pound. Mr. Pound looked at the Elizabeth Star for some time, then looked up at Mr. Evans. "I guess we'd both better talk to the police," he said.

"I think it would be the right thing to do," said Henry.

"I think if you confess," Grandfather put in, "you'll be able to work something out so you don't go to jail. After all, you haven't yet actually reported it missing to your insurance company, have you?"

Mr. Pound shook his head. "No, I haven't."

Grandfather went on, "And Mr. Evans here did cooperate, finally. If *you* don't press charges against him perhaps the police will drop the case. . . ."

When Mr. Pound had left, Jessie said to Mr. Evans, "Thanks for your help in solving the mystery."

"Glad to do it," said Mr. Evans. "An honest electrician, that's me." He emphasized the word *honest* and added, "From now on."

"Good," said Violet, smiling at him.

"Hey, I saw the light," said Mr. Evans. "That's a joke."

"In the chandelier?" asked Benny, puzzled.

Everyone laughed. And, as usual, Benny laughed, too, although he wasn't quite sure why everyone was laughing.

The Aldens spent their last day in New York City hunting for souvenirs and packing. By late afternoon they were waiting in the lobby with Mrs. Teague for the hired car that would take them to the train station when the elevator doors slid silently open.

"Look out," cried a familiar voice. And out came Lydia into the hall. But this time, she didn't have five French bulldogs on a leash. She had a huge Irish wolfhound.

"Woof," said Watch, and stopped, unsure of himself. Even he had never seen a dog that big.

"Don't worry. Erin — that's her name — is very friendly," said Lydia, pulling on the leash.

Erin sat down.

"Is Erin one of your new dog clients?" asked Violet.

"Yep. And guess what? I just got a part in a new play. *Diamonds and Hearts*. On Broadway!" said Lydia.

"Congratulations," all the Aldens said at once.

"You'll have to come see it. It opens at Christmas. And you know why I got the part?" she went on.

"Your lucky crystal?" asked Henry.

"Well, that, maybe. And the dog who has a starring role liked me!" Lydia beamed. "I guess it's all my experience with dogs. Critt's Critters is going to make me a star!"

Erin stood up.

"Okay," Lydia said to Erin.

"Lydia," said Jessie quickly, "a few nights ago, after you walked the French bulldogs, you stayed upstairs a long time. What happened?"

Lydia thought a moment, then grinned. "Jill got away, out in the hall. It took me almost twenty minutes to catch her, the little rascal."

"Another mystery solved," said Jessie, grinning.

"Speaking of mysteries," said Lydia, "did you hear about Mr. Pound? It's in all the papers. His stolen diamond was found and he's going to donate it to the Museum of Natural History. Can you imagine giving such a valuable thing away? I bet there's a story behind *that* news item!"

"I bet there is," said Henry, and the children exchanged smiles.

At that moment, Lydia noticed the luggage for the first time. "You're leaving?" she said.

"It's time to go home," Grandfather Alden said.

Mr. Saunders came in. "Your car is ready," he said.

"Come back soooon," Lydia said as Erin the wolfhound pulled her through the door.

"Yes, come back soon," said Mrs. Teague. She hugged everybody, even Watch.

And Mr. Saunders actually waved as the hired car pulled away from the building.

Violet sighed as she looked out of the window of the train. The lights of New York City stretched across the skyline.

"Like diamonds," said Benny, looking out over her shoulder.

"We had fun, didn't we?" said Henry.

"Yes," said Violet. "I hope we come back."

Grandfather, who was sitting across the aisle, heard Violet. "I guess New York doesn't seem so big now, does it, Violet?"

"It's still big," said Violet. "But most of the people are pretty nice."

"Don't worry," said Benny. "We'll be back. There are about a million mysteries in a big city like New York. And somebody's got to solve them."

Violet smiled. "Who else? The Alden Family Detective Agency, of course."

GERTRUDE CHANDLER WARNER discovered when she was teaching that many readers who like an exciting story could find no books that were both easy and fun to read. She decided to try to meet this need, and her first book, *The Boxcar Children*, quickly proved she had succeeded.

Miss Warner drew on her own experiences to write the mystery. As a child she spent hours watching trains go by on the tracks opposite her family home. She often dreamed about what it would be like to set up housekeeping in a caboose or freight car—the situation the Alden children find themselves in.

While the mystery element is central to each of Miss Warner's books, she never thought of them as strictly juvenile mysteries. She liked to stress the Aldens' independence and resourcefulness and their solid New England devotion to using up and making do. The Aldens go about most of their adventures with as little adult supervision as possible—something else that delights young readers.

Miss Warner lived in Putnam, Connecticut, until her death in 1979. During her lifetime, she received hundreds of letters from girls and boys telling her how much they liked her books.

New York, New York!

The Aldens are on their way to visit a big city —
New York City! What will they find there? The
Statue of Liberty? The Empire State Building?
Central Park? Yellow taxis? Well, they probably
will find all of those things and more. Knowing the
Boxcar Children, they'll also probably find a mys-
tery or two along the way.

Now you can find some puzzling mysteries, too.
Just grab your pencils and get started on the puz-
zles and games on the next few pages. You can
check your answers on pages 137–38. Good luck,
detectives — you're in for a ride that's as wild as a
ride in a yellow taxi!

Taxi!

Oh, no! Lydia, one of the Boxcar Children's main suspects, is getting away. Henry, Jessie, Violet, and Benny quickly jump into a taxi and speed through the streets of Manhattan. Can you help the taxicab driver navigate the streets so Lydia doesn't get away?

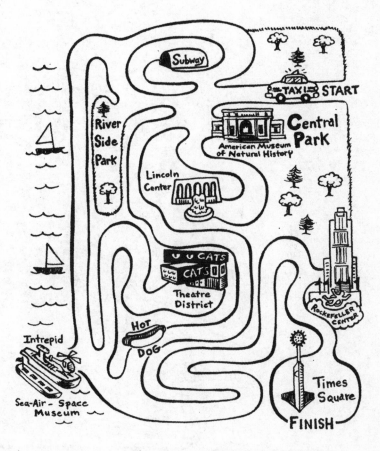

A Walk in the Park

The Boxcar Children are taking a walk in Central Park. Color in this scene any way you want. Try to remember everything you see. Then turn the page and circle the correct answers on the memory test.

Test your memory by answering these questions:

1. The woman wearing headphones is:
   a) sitting on a bench b) eating a hot dog
   c) jogging d) walking a dog
2. How many passengers (besides the driver) is the horse and carriage carrying?
   a) two b) four c) six d) eight
3. The man wearing shorts is:
   a) wheeling a baby carriage b) biking
   c) walking d) reading the newspaper
4. Who is in-line skating?
   a) a boy wearing jeans b) a woman wearing a hat c) a girl with long hair d) a man with a dog
5. What is the man on the bench doing?
   a) feeding pigeons b) reading the newspaper
   c) sleeping d) talking to a friend
6. How many dogs is the woman walking?
   a) one b) three c) five d) six
7. What type of food is being sold in the park?
   a) pizza b) pretzels c) hot dogs d) hamburgers

Precious Diamond

The Elizabeth Star is a very famous and valuable diamond pendant. It's one of a kind. And now it's missing! There are ten diamond pendants in this picture, but only one is the Elizabeth Star. Can you guess which one it is? It is different from the rest.

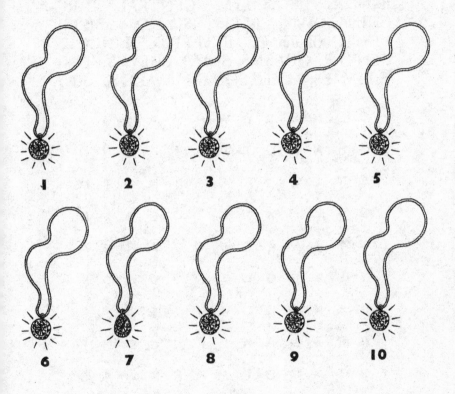

Sightseeing

The Boxcar Children have a long list of sights they want to see when they're in New York. Can you help them find the attractions in this word search? The words go up, down, sideways, backward, and diagonally. Look for: BOWERY, BROADWAY, BRONX, BROOKLYN, CENTRAL PARK, CHINATOWN, ELLIS ISLAND, EMPIRE STATE (Building), INTREPID, LINCOLN CENTER, QUEENS, SOHO, SUBWAY, TAXI, TIFFANYS, TIMES SQUARE, WALL STREET.

```
C E N S U B W A Y A W O S
H E N W O T A N I H C N O
C T C E N R L A R K E T D
E A O N X T L I B E B I N
N T I M E S S Q U A R E A
T S K B O O T Q U D O S L
R E X H O O R U I I A Y S
A R O N A W E P X Q D N I
L I X O O E E A R K W A S
P P O Z O R T R P A A F I
A M C E T R B A Y L Y F L
R E T N E C N L O C N I L
K R I B R O O K L Y N T E
```

Tangled Leashes

Oh, no! Lydia Critt of Critt's Critters was out in Central Park taking the dogs for a walk when their leashes got tangled. Can you help her untangle the leashes? Follow the dogs' leashes and match each dog's name with a number.

Broadway, Broadway

Broadway is the only street that runs through Manhattan from top to bottom. Broadway is one *long* street! And you can make a lot of *smaller* words from the word BROADWAY, too. Henry made 28 three-, four-, and five-letter words. See how many you can make.

BROADWAY

_____   _____   _____

_____   _____   _____

_____   _____   _____

_____   _____   _____

_____   _____   _____

_____   _____   _____

_____   _____   _____

_____   _____   _____

_____   _____   _____

A Souvenir

The Boxcar Children bought a souvenir poster of Manhattan. But when they unwrap their poster, it doesn't look right. Look at the poster below and cross out the places that don't belong.

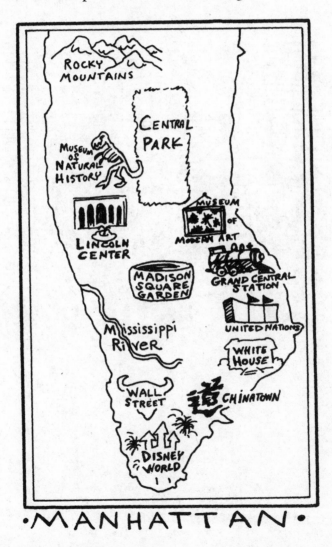

ROCKY MOUNTAINS

CENTRAL PARK

MUSEUM OF NATURAL HISTORY

LINCOLN CENTER

MUSEUM OF MODERN ART

MADISON SQUARE GARDEN

GRAND CENTRAL STATION

UNITED NATIONS

Mississippi River

WHITE HOUSE

WALL STREET

CHINATOWN

DISNEY WORLD

· MANHATTAN ·

Hot Dog Hunt

Hot dogs are a delicious New York treat. You can find a vendor on practically every corner in the city! There are ten hot dogs hidden in the picture below. Circle the ones you find.

A Yummy New York Treat

The Boxcar Children are very tired and hungry from running around New York City all day. It's a perfect time to find a New York coffee shop and have a snack! They go inside, hop up on the stools at the counter, and order four famous New York egg creams. Sounds good? Well, now you can make your own egg cream at home. Just follow these simple steps:

Ingredients:
1 cup milk
Seltzer (it's best if you use seltzer from a pressurized bottle because it has lots of fizz)
2 tablespoons chocolate syrup

Directions: Pour 1 cup of milk into a 12-ounce glass. Top with some seltzer so that the white foam reaches the top of the glass. Place spoon into the glass. Pour 2 tablespoons of chocolate syrup into the glass, hitting the bottom of the spoon if possible. Stir quickly to blend the syrup into the milk. Pop in straw, and drink immediately!
Note: You can use vanilla syrup for a vanilla egg cream.

After drinking their egg creams, the Boxcar Children found a mystery! Where are the eggs in the egg cream? Here's what they found out:

A candy shop owner named Louis Auster invented the egg cream in 1890 in Brooklyn, New York. His egg creams were so popular that lines of people would form down the street and around the corner from his store. But he never told anyone his secret recipe.

One theory is that Louis Auster's egg cream contained both eggs and cream, but that once it was discovered that raw eggs were unsafe to eat, they were eliminated. Another theory is that the chocolate syrup was made with eggs and cream, and that's how the drink got its name.

And the final theory is that the drink just tasted like it had eggs and cream in it, so it was named egg cream!

Answers:

Taxi!

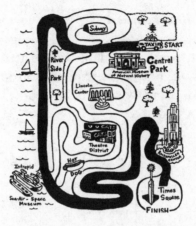

A Walk in the Park: 1. c; 2. a; 3. b; 4. c; 5. a; 6. d; 7. b

Precious Diamond: The Elizabeth Star is #7.

Sightseeing

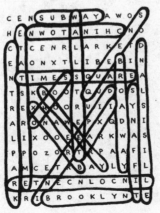

Tangled Leashes: Jim is #1. Jack is #2. Joe is #3. Jill is #4. Jinx is #5.

Broadway, Broadway

Possible answers: bad, dab, wad, bay, day, ray, way, bar, oar, war, bow, row, raw, boy, rod, orb, bard, ward, yard, drab, draw, boar, body, brow, road, away, wary, broad

A Souvenir

Hot Dog Hunt